To
Sean
Love Ya Papa
Nana + Papa
2003

Flavia and Her Fabulous Friends

Flavia and Her Fabulous Friends

By Daniel Percheron

Illustrated by Christian Vassort

ABBEVILLE KIDS
A Division of Abbeville Publishing Group
New York   London   Paris

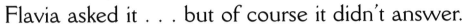lavia lived a very ordinary life with her family, in the quietest part of the city. Right across the street was a park with a zoo inside. There was even an aviary full of birds!

Flavia had a goldfish that was not so ordinary. When the goldfish was very little, it had jumped out of its bowl right into Flavia's glass of limeade! "What are you doing?" Flavia asked it . . . but of course it didn't answer.

Flavia put the goldfish back in its bowl, but not before it turned the color of limeade: bright green! Nobody ever figured out why the goldfish had jumped out of its bowl.

Actually, Flavia was not so ordinary either. She never slept in the house—she could only sleep on four wheels. Even when she was very small, her mother said, Flavia couldn't sleep a wink unless she was in her baby carriage.

Every evening, Flavia wished her family good night and walked out the front door. She went straight to the family's little blue mini-van, which was parked along the sidewalk. The mini-van was not a bad place to spend the night, dreaming beautiful dreams.

Often Flavia whistled a soft tune to the birds in the zoo. She hoped she was whistling, "Sleep tight!"

Each morning, at sunrise, the birds in the park started singing songs of their own. Flavia always woke up to this outdoor concert. She listened to the different birdsongs from under her covers. "I wish I knew what those birds were singing about," she sighed to herself.

When Flavia left the blue mini-van, she often met her neighbor Lucas Topsy-Turvy. He loved to walk upside-down along the sidewalk. Lucas tended to sulk whenever he had to walk in any other way.

Flavia enjoyed these early meetings. Whenever she saw Lucas coming down the sidewalk with his feet up in the air, she waved to him. Then Lucas would stop and say hi to her feet!

When Flavia came through the
front door of her house, she always
remembered to feed her green goldfish.
Flavia fed it green peas each and every morning.
She thought they were good for its complexion.

Flavia sat at the breakfast table with her brother Victor.
He wore stripes all year 'round—in summer, winter, spring,
and fall. He wore a striped shirt during the day, and striped
pajamas at night. If Victor wore anything that didn't have
stripes, he got round spots on his back!

As he ate, Victor wondered when his sister was going
to get tired of sleeping in the same old little blue mini-van.
Flavia wondered when her brother would get tired of
wearing the same old striped pajamas.

At school, Flavia sat next to Julie Dogwood. Julie barely paid attention in class. Instead, she spent her time learning the names of all the flowers outside the school window by heart.

All those flower names made Julie's eyes feel heavy, so she needed to wear glasses. Flavia's ears were often full of the birdsongs she heard early in the morning, but her head did not feel heavy.

Maybe, Flavia thought, it was because she didn't know the names of all those great singers! Flavia decided that she ought to take a closer look at the birds in the zoo.

The very next morning, Flavia awoke earlier than usual in her little blue mini-van. The moon was still full, so she stayed under her covers for a while and whistled to herself. But soon she got tired of waiting.

It was time to investigate! Flavia climbed into the park through a hole in the fence. Now she would be able to visit the birds of the zoo up close, without being disturbed.

First she went to the corner where the owls were. The fisher owl, which sat on a perch over the pond, suddenly went KOO-oo-KOO-KOO. Then Flavia noticed the spectacled owl, hiding in a hole in a tree. "Hmph!" she said. "Those two black circles around its eyes look just like Julie Dogwood's glasses!"

Flavia left the owls corner, passed two sleeping monkeys, and soon found herself next to a large aviary, filled with every kind of bird. Just what she was looking for!

Up above, the moon was disappearing in the pale sky. Sunrise was near. The birds were starting to sing, and Flavia did not know which way to go.

Then she saw the blackbirds. The backs of their heads were yellow, like caps worn backwards. Their little orange beaks let out all kinds of sharp little chirps. Suddenly, Flavia heard one of them say, "This is boring. This is boring."

"This is boring. This is boring"—the message was clear.

"Of course," Flavia said aloud, "it can't be any fun to be in a cage all the time, doing the same things over and over, every day and every night." There were so many other interesting things to do and see!

Flavia decided to learn more about this blackbird. What could she do to help it? Quickly, she made her way back out through the fence.

Flavia returned home, and fed her fish its peas. Today it didn't eat the peas as quickly as usual. Flavia suddenly realized that it, too, might be bored with its bowl. Was that why it had jumped into her limeade? Could it now be tired of the green peas, too? "Maybe I'll try feeding you something new," Flavia whispered to her goldfish.

Flavia was making herself a cup of hot chocolate in the kitchen when her brother made his entrance. Victor stretched as much as he could. He enjoyed hearing his bones crack in his striped pajamas.

Those stripes reminded Flavia of the bars on the blackbird's cage. How strange, she thought. Bars made the bird bored while stripes made Victor happy. But Flavia shook off her deep thoughts. "Hey, Victor," she said, "I just met a talking bird!"

Victor stared at her as if she were crazy.

"I mean it!" insisted Flavia. "Come help me investigate."
She walked over to the encyclopedia. Victor usually stayed far
away from the bookshelf, but he couldn't believe that Flavia
had really met a talking bird! She must have been dreaming.

Flavia and Victor looked up **B** for blackbird. It took
them a little time to find out that
Flavia's blackbird came from

Malaysia . . . and it really **could** imitate human speech!
"I guess you weren't dreaming," Victor said.

Victor started to look interested. He dove into the
encyclopedia again, looking under the letter **M**. Malaysia was
very far away, where there were pineapples, coconuts, and
palm trees. Flavia had no trouble imagining her blackbird
flying among the coconut trees, showing no signs of boredom.

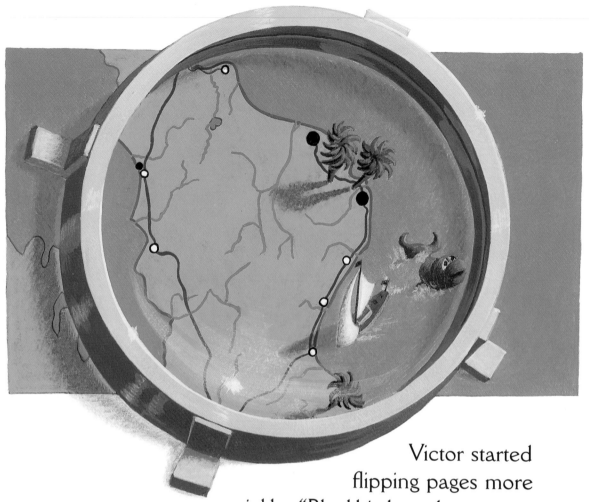

Victor started
flipping pages more
quickly. "Blackbirds and coconut trees
are all very well," he said, "but I want to know where
Malaysia is **exactly**." He dove for a third time into the
encyclopedia, looking for a map.

Sitting next to him on the arm of the chair, Flavia
suddenly saw the green fish start swimming in very peculiar
circles! Just as Victor put his finger on the little drawing of
Malaysia, Flavia grabbed his sleeve. "Look!" she cried.

In utter astonishment, they watched as the green fish
jumped high in the air! It did three loopity-loops by waving
its fins, and then—with a flip of its tail—splashed back into
the bowl.

"Apparently," said Victor, "that was enough fresh air."

At recess that day, Flavia stood under the tree whistling, while she puzzled over what she could do to help the blackbird.

But suddenly, to Flavia's surprise, Julie Dogwood shouted, "No more flowers! It's time for a change!" She tossed her glasses to Flavia and hurled

herself into the basketball game. She played until she was dizzy. And finally, it was clear to see, her head did **not** feel heavy!

Lucas Topsy-Turvy walked over to Flavia, on his feet; walking upside-down was not allowed at school. He looked very glum, so Flavia told him about the blackbird.

"I know what we can do," he interrupted her. "Let's put on a show for the bird! We'll give it something new to think about!" Flavia agreed—what a great idea! Lucas wasn't glum anymore.

In the background, they could hear Julie Dogwood laughing from the basketball court: "Way cool!" they heard her shout. "Way Cool! WAY COOL!"

The next morning, Flavia and Lucas crept into the zoo at the crack of dawn. As soon as Flavia spotted the blackbird, she began to whistle at the top of her lungs.

Immediately the blackbird opened its eyes! Lucas flipped upside-down and began to dance, hopping and twirling on his hands. The blackbird squawked and flapped its wings wildly. And then they heard it: the blackbird was **talking!**

"Way cool. Way Cool! WAY COOL!" it squawked.

Suddenly, Flavia understood. What had Victor read from the encyclopedia? Her blackbird could **imitate human speech**. "Lucas, stop," she said quietly. "When the blackbird said it was bored, it was just repeating what someone at the zoo said! It didn't mean anything." Lucas sadly put his feet back down on the ground.

But suddenly he smiled. "That doesn't mean we have to stop our show!" he cried. He flipped back onto his hands and started dancing again, with more jumps and twirls than ever. He even started to whistle! "He's right!" thought Flavia. With a gigantic laugh, she, too, began to whistle, and danced a little jig herself.

From the blackbird's cage, Flavia and Lucas were sure they heard the sounds of the blackbird laughing, too.

Flavia got home just in time to feed her goldfish its breakfast. As she walked through the front door, Victor looked up from the book he had just started reading. "So," he asked his sister, "what did you find out at the zoo?"

Flavia noticed that Victor was wearing a shirt covered with red polka-dots, and yet he didn't have any spots on his back. "Oh," she answered, turning toward her bedroom— where she might try sleeping that night, she decided—"just that we all need a change, every once in a while."

With that, she smiled at her green goldfish, and walked away. With a flip of its tail, the goldfish smiled back.

For Clara

Editor: Leslie Bockol

Designer: Jordana Abrams

Production Editor: Meredith Wolf

Production Manager: Lou Bilka

First edition

2 4 6 8 10 9 7 5 3 1

Library of Congress Cataloging-in-Publication Data
Percheron, Daniel.
Flavia and her fabulous friends / by Daniel Percheron ;
illustrated by Christian Vassort.
p. cm.
Summary: Flavia and all her friends are very particular about what they
like and dislike, but one day, after a talking bird says that it's bored, she
decides maybe everyone needs a change once in a while.
ISBN 0-7892-0302-2
[1. Cats—Fiction. 2. Animals—Fiction. 3. Change—Fiction.]
I. Vassort, Christian, ill. II. Title.
PZ7.P423F1   1997
[E]—dc21   97-34844